Dedicated to
all the children of the world,
whom we thank God for.

Thankful Hearts
Wonderful World

Illustrations by
Marco Zerneri

Story by
Ty Stover

In a world where wonders are abundant,
children are waking in their beds.

As the golden rays stretch across the sky,
they open their arms wide and say,

"Thank you, SUN,
for the warmth on my face."

"Thank you, CLOUDS, for the water that makes the flowers grow."

"Thank you,
TREES,
for giving the birds
a place to sing
and
build their nests."

"Thank you,
OCEAN,
for your rhythmic waves
that soothe our souls
and inspire our dreams."

"Thank you, WIND, for your gentle push that makes the world dance."

"Thank you, MOUNTAINS, for standing strong and filling our hearts with awe."

"Thank you, SNOWFLAKES, for turning the world into a magical wonderland."

"Thank you,
MOON,
for creating the tides
that dance along
the shoreline."

"Thank you, STARS,
for lighting up the night
and
making wishes come true."

As the seasons change
and the world transforms...

"Thank you,
WORLD,
for all the wonders
that make each day special."

And at night as they pray in their bed,
they always remember the most important
'thank you' of all,

"Thank you,
GOD,
for creating it all
for us."

From the sun's warmth to the moon's glow,
from the rain's song to the trees' embrace,
know that every part of the world
is God's gift to be cherished.

A reminder that in every corner of the world,
there are countless reasons to say,

"Thank you"

Thankful Hearts: Wonderful World © 2024 Ty Stover

All rights reserved.

Story by Ty Stover
Illustrations, Layout & graphic design by Marco Zerneri for TACOM - Creative Studio

ISBN 979-8-35094-206-4